MW00952409

The Best Kind of Day

Written by Kathleen Gwilliam • Illustrated by Ayan Saha

CFI · An imprint of Cedar Fort, Inc. · Springville, Utah

Today was a really good day.
The best I've ever had.
Everything was perfect.
Not one little thing went bad.

I woke up to the smell of bacon
Sizzling in the pan.
And then I saw Mom's pancakes!
Yes, that's how my day began.

I was the first one on the bus,
So I got the best seat,
The one that sends you flying from
The speed bumps on the street.

I had studied very hard
For my spelling test today.
I got every single word right!
Teacher put it on display.

At lunch, Jake shared his treat with me.
It was coconut supreme!
At recess I was picked to be
The head of my kickball team.

Tonight at my softball game
We were tied at the last inning.
I hit the ball clear out of the park.
The game ended with us winning!

Dad got home early and
Surprised me with a hat.
One that's pink and sparkly with
A glittery baseball bat.

After dinner we had family night.
I got to pick the treat.
We made Gran's chocolate brownies.
They were ooey gooey sweet!

"Dear Father in Heaven,
Thank you for this perfect day.
I can't wait until tomorrow.
Make it just as good, I pray!"

"Wake up! Wake up, Jamie!
We're going to be late.
Breakfast is on the table.
Get dressed and grab your plate!"

Mom seems very frazzled,
So I get dressed real quick.
What! Burnt toast and a glass of milk?
This has to be a trick.

"I didn't want this orange juice.
It has the yucky pulp!"
"Here, Karl, you can have my milk."
I drink the juice in one big gulp.

"My rain boots have a hole in them!"
My little sister cried.
"Hattie, you can wear my boots.
I'll walk carefully outside."

We run out to the car since
We missed the bus today.
Hattie jumps into a puddle
And makes the water spray.

Water is dripping down my neck.
My morning's not been great.
I hope that when I get to school
I'll meet a better fate.

We pull up as we hear the bell.
I dash to get inside.
Suddenly I trip and fall.
My shoelace is untied!

Oh great! My jeans now have a hole.
They are my favorite pair!
"Jamie, you are tardy.
Please quickly find your chair."

While doing our map worksheet,
My friend is stressed, I see.
"Look down at the bottom
And just follow the key."

"Jamie, there's no talking.
You must do your work alone.
Pull your desk off to the side
In the timeout zone."

PE time is finally here.
Things might be getting better.
I love playing volleyball,
Especially when I'm setter.

Miranda never hits the ball,
But it goes over the net!
I could bump it, but I let her score,
And now my team's upset.

"This day just needs to end," I say
As we walk to the bus stop.
"All day long I've had bad luck,
Like one big belly flop!"

Suddenly a ball rolls past
And off of the concrete.
Hattie chases after it
And runs into the street!

I drop my bag and pull her back
Just as a car drives by.
My backpack landed in a puddle.
I hope my homework's dry!

"Dear daughter,
today was not bad
If you see it
through my eyes.
It was a
really good day.
I saw so many highs.

Your mom was running late. I saw you help her out.
You gave things to your siblings that You'd rather kept, no doubt.

You were aware of people Who were struggling today.
Time and time again I saw Your true love on display.

You put others first, my child,
And recognized their needs.
Even when those around you
Would not be very pleased.

Today you helped my children,
Showing your love for me.
Inasmuch as ye have done it unto
One of the least of these . . .

Ye have done it unto me!

I promise you that your idea
Of good days will come.
But as far as I'm concerned,
Today was the best one."

To Mom and Dad,
who taught me what a good day looked like
—Kathie

Text © 2020 Kathleen Gwilliam
Illustrations © 2020 Ayan Saha
All rights reserved.

No part of this book may be reproduced in any form whatsoever, whether by graphic, visual, electronic, film, microfilm, tape recording, or any other means, without prior written permission of the publisher, except in the case of brief passages embodied in critical reviews and articles.

This is not an official publication of The Church of Jesus Christ of Latter-day Saints. The opinions and views expressed herein belong solely to the author and do not necessarily represent the opinions or views of Cedar Fort, Inc. Permission for the use of sources, graphics, and photos is also solely the responsibility of the author.

ISBN 13: 978-1-4621-3613-1

Published by CFI, an imprint of Cedar Fort, Inc.
2373 W. 700 S., Springville, UT 84663
Distributed by Cedar Fort, Inc., www.cedarfort.com

Library of Congress Control Number: 2020933729

Cover design and typesetting by Shawnda T. Craig
Cover design © 2020 Cedar Fort, Inc.

Printed in the United States of America

10 9 8 7 6 5 4 3 2 1

Printed on acid-free paper